A SUDDEN STORM

Dennis Fertig • Illustrated by Scott Goto

STECK-VAUGHN
ELEMENTARY · SECONDARY · ADULT · LIBRARY

A Harcourt Company

www.steck-vaughn.com

ISBN 0-7398-5102-0

Printed in China.

4 5 6 7 8 9 LB 06 05 04 03

CONTENTS

CHAPTER 1

AT THE CAMPFIRE

A flaming arrow flew across the night sky. It hit a large pile of carefully stacked logs. In moments, the logs were blazing. Camp Outback's campfire night had begun.

Michael liked the way the counselors started the fire. It was cool. But he didn't tell anybody that. After all, he was 13, and this was his third summer at Camp Outback. He had seen the flaming arrow trick before. Plus, he was a city kid from Detroit. City kids didn't say out loud that anything was cool.

"Cool!" said Tyler, who sat next to him.

Michael smiled. Tyler was a city kid who was impressed by stuff and willing to show it. Michael was only a year older than Tyler, but sometimes Tyler seemed even younger.

Camp Outback was a summer place for Detroit city boys. It was on the shore of East Lake, deep in the wilderness of upper Michigan. During the past two summers, Michael had come here for two weeks. He had met Tyler here last year.

Down by the fire, Mr. Bell said, "Welcome to the 'Save Our Lake' campfire." Mr. Bell used to be a Detroit police officer. He ran the camp.

The campfire was in the middle of an outdoor area at the bottom of a hill. Kids sat on log seats cut into the hill like stairs.

Michael and Tyler were sitting high up on the hill. The moon was shining brightly, and they could see East Lake clearly. Michael couldn't make himself look at the water, though. ⚡

"Get ready!" Mr. Bell said. "We'll have you clapping along to songs about East Lake. Then, we'll have some skits performed by Cabin B. Finally, we'll give out some neat prizes for the best 'Save Our Lake' crafts."

Michael rolled his eyes. Saving the lake was important, but this other stuff was boring. Plays, songs, posters, and crafts were not what Michael was all about.

"Cool," Tyler whispered. "I hope my totem pole wins."

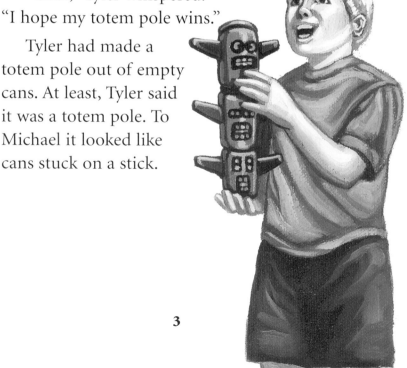

Tyler had made a totem pole out of empty cans. At least, Tyler said it was a totem pole. To Michael it looked like cans stuck on a stick.

"Later, we'll announce the 'Save Our Lake' canoeists," Mr. Bell said.

Every summer, campers from Camp Outback teamed up with kids from Wilderness Bay Camp, a nearby girls' camp. Together, they cleaned public campsites around East Lake. Most kids had to hike to the sites. But the two best canoeists from each camp canoed to campsites far across the lake. Cleaning up trash wasn't much fun, but being picked to canoe to the campsites was a real honor.

"Michael, that's us," Tyler whispered. "We're the best canoeists in camp."

"You've got that right," Michael replied. But as he did, his stomach tightened. Last year, he had wanted to be chosen more than anything. He was a strong swimmer and one of the best canoeists in camp. When he wasn't picked, he was disappointed.

That was last year. This year, Michael had a secret. No one at camp knew about it. Everyone thought Michael loved swimming and canoeing. No one noticed that this summer he'd found lots of reasons to skip swimming. In canoeing classes, he did well but he was nervous.

The campfire evening lasted for two hours. Some songs and plays were funny. Some were even silly. Tyler enjoyed them all, but none took Michael's fears away.

When the prizes for best posters and crafts were handed out, Tyler didn't win. He didn't mind, though, because a few minutes later Mr. Bell said something that made him very happy.

Mr. Bell announced in a booming voice, "The 'Save Our Lake' canoeists this year are Tyler McNeill and Michael Cameron."

As Tyler yelled, Michael looked fearfully at the lake. He had owned this lake for the last two summers. He'd had no fears. But tomorrow he would have to canoe across it, and the thought terrified him.

CHAPTER 2

A BAD NIGHT, AGAIN

Long after the campfire ended, Michael lay awake. Tyler was sound asleep. Michael envied his tent mate. He wished he could sleep, but all he could do was watch as his memory kept playing the tape of that horrible spring night over and over.

Click. The tape started again.

It was a hot, sticky night in May. Michael and his friends thought they would cool off in a public swimming pool. It wasn't summer, so the pool wasn't open. That didn't worry them.

Michael and Rondell were the first ones over the fence. Then came Ted, Barry, and Keshawn.

On the other side, the boys stopped in the dark. They waited to see if lights went on, alarms sounded, or dogs came barking. Nothing happened.

They checked the pool. It was full of water. Rondell said, "Good! It's filled!"

As the boys took off their shoes and socks, their eyes got used to the darkness. They got a better look at the water.

"That's not pool water," Keshawn said. "It's dirty rain water." The water was mixed with leaves, cans, and other junk.

"Forget this," Michael said.

They started to put their shoes on when a police car drove by. It stopped. A police officer shone a spotlight on them. The boys took off.

Michael didn't get far. He tripped and fell into the dirty water. On the way in, he hit his head on the side of the pool. He was stunned. He sank to the bottom of the deep end.

Michael was lucky. Police officer Diane Brown was watching. In a heartbeat, she was out of the car and over the fence. With her flashlight, she searched the dark water. She couldn't see Michael. She grabbed the radio from her equipment belt and called for help. Then she took the belt off and jumped feet first into the pool.

Maybe it was Officer Brown's splash, or maybe it was the cold water, but something brought Michael back.

His eyes popped open. He was conscious, but where was he? He opened his mouth to breathe and drank in dirty water.

Michael panicked. He kicked wildly. His foot hit the bottom of the pool and pushed him up. In a few moments, his head broke through the surface of the water. Michael opened his mouth again and breathed in a little air, a few leaves, and a lot more dirty water.

He coughed and choked. He stretched toward the edge of the pool but he couldn't reach it.

Michael sank back under the water. He tried to struggle to the surface, but his thrashing movements forced him down. His lungs screamed for air.

He grabbed wildly for something to hang on to, but that made things worse. Michael was sure he was going to die.

Then, he felt a strong tug at the back of his shirt collar. He felt another tug and his head was above water. Another tug and he was at the edge of the pool. Michael was coughing and gasping for air, but he was alive.

Officer Brown had pulled him out.

Click. End of tape.

As Michael lay awake, he knew he was being too hard on himself. The only reason he had almost drowned in that pool was because

he had been knocked out. But he couldn't forget the crushing feeling of not being able to breathe and the horrible, choking taste of the dirty water. Could he put his fear aside and climb into that canoe tomorrow?

The next morning was beautiful, bright, and sunny. The sky and the lake seemed to be having a contest to see which could be the bluest. But Michael, still sleepy from a night of fear, was disappointed. Rain and storms would have been better. Then it would be too dangerous to go out on East Lake.

After breakfast, he and Tyler met Mr. Bell and Jeremy Sellars at the dock. Jeremy was the Camp Outback canoe counselor who would go with them across the lake today. In a few moments, a van from Wilderness Bay Camp pulled up.

The Camp Outback group shook hands with Ms. Sanders, the head of the girls' camp. They said hello to Amy Loo, the canoe counselor, and two campers, Eva Sanchez and Kara Elison. Michael knew the girls from the last two summers. Both were super canoeists.

After a little talk, the canoeists put on life jackets and climbed into the canoes. The counselors split up. Amy joined Tyler in one canoe, while Jeremy and Kara were in the second. Michael and Eva shared the third canoe.

When Michael stepped into his canoe, he felt clumsy and nervous.

He was sure Eva could tell he was afraid. If she did, she didn't say anything. Mr. Bell gave their canoe a push off the shore. "Have a safe trip," he said.

That was all Michael hoped for. But what if something went wrong?

CHAPTER 3

A GOOD START

Michael was in the stern of the canoe. Being in the back meant he had to do most of the steering. This was where most of the skill was needed. He wished he could be in the front. He knew Eva could handle the stern well, and besides, he was so nervous. But teamwork was important in canoeing. Steering was Michael's job now, and he had to do his part.

At first it was a challenge. Michael was so worried that he made a few mistakes. Eva stared at him over her shoulder. But in a few minutes, he was doing okay. Eva turned and looked at him. "That's better, Michael," she said. "You scared me at first."

"My mind was somewhere else," he said. He didn't add, *It was screaming for help at the bottom of a dark pool.*

Keeping the canoe moving forward was the easy part. Keeping his stomach calm was the hard part. The thought of water below them, deep water, terrified Michael. If he panicked in this water, he could sink and never come back up.

Before the canoeists were too far from shore, Amy gave them the plan for the day. "Our first stop will be a campsite just north and east of Camp Outback," she explained. "It should take us 45 minutes to get there. We'll give ourselves an hour to clean it up."

That was good news for Michael. It meant they were cutting across one corner of the lake. They would never be too far from shore.

Amy went on, "Then we'll canoe to the second campsite. That will take an hour or so. We'll clean up the camp and have lunch there."

Michael knew the way to the second campsite meant they would be near shore again.

"How will we get back to Camp Outback?" Kara asked.

"Straight across the lake," Jeremy answered. ⚡

Eva, Tyler, and Kara cheered. Paddling across the lake was the kind of challenge good canoeists love. The kids knew that some years, the best canoeists in camp weren't good enough to get the chance to do it.

Michael's fears deepened. The lake was calm now, but who knew what it would be like after lunch? If something happened to the canoes in the middle of the lake, there would be no shore nearby. Michael was so worried, that at first he didn't hear Tyler calling him.

"Michael," Tyler was saying. "Your Detroit friends will never believe this. City kids like us paddling across this deep lake!"

"It's no big deal," Michael said in his coolest voice. "Bet I don't even tell them." ⚡

"Bet you do!" Tyler yelled.

Michael only hoped he lived through this trip to tell them.

Eva said, "Michael, you're playing it too cool. You know you love it out here."

The strange thing was that Eva was right. Once they were moving, Michael started to enjoy the lake. Eva was a good canoeist. She used a steady, powerful stroke. Michael matched her. They raced through the water. Soon their canoe was ahead of the other two.

Their speed and teamwork, plus the beauty and quiet of the lake, helped Michael relax.

After 45 minutes of paddling, the canoes docked at the first campsite. The six canoeists then cleaned the campsite carefully, stuffing paper, cans, and other junk into plastic trash bags. When they filled a bag, they tied it and left it by the road that led to the site. Later, park rangers would come and collect the bags.

The kids were amazed at the garbage that had been left. Michael and Tyler had seen some city neighborhoods that were littered with trash. They had seen walls and alleys covered with graffiti. Back home, both boys treasured the memory of how clean East Lake and the forest were.

The canoes were soon back in the water and on their way to the second campsite. Michael felt even better now. He and Eva trailed behind. The canoes ahead glided along, leaving little ripples behind them. The green of the shore, the blue of the sky and lake, and the paddles flashing in the sun all painted a wonderful picture.

"Cool," Michael said, almost under his breath. Eva looked back at him in surprise.

Maybe today will be okay after all, Michael thought. Just then, he noticed small waves in the lake. The water was choppier than before.

CHAPTER 4

A SCARY STORY

The crews landed at the second campsite. They cleaned up the area and then sat down to lunch. Michael noticed that Tyler had a plastic bag of empty cans and several long pieces of rope.

"What's that?" Michael asked.

"Junk I found," Tyler said. "I'm going to use it to make a 'Save Our Lake' craft."

Tyler was always looking for ways to reuse things people threw away. That's one reason Michael liked him.

"What will you make?" Kara asked.

"I don't know yet," Tyler grinned.

"Don't lose that junk in my lake," Michael kidded.

Tyler's eyes got bigger. "That makes me think of something that happened here years ago," he said.

"You mean when those five or six people drowned?" Kara asked.

Michael didn't want to hear this.

"Right. Six men went out on a nice day like this. But it turned stormy. They tipped over their canoes in the storm," Tyler said.

"What happened?" Eva asked.

"After the storm, the police found three canoes in the middle of the lake. Two were upside-down. Floating around the canoes were a bunch of empty cans," Tyler answered. "Over the next few days, five bodies washed up in Wilderness Bay. The last body was never found. It's still somewhere deep in the lake."

No one said anything for a moment.

"They were probably doing something stupid," Michael said loudly.

"Maybe," Jeremy said. He looked at Amy.

"Look, Tyler," she said. "I don't know if that old story is true. But this lake can be hard on anybody in a storm."

Michael's terror was stronger than ever. He couldn't eat his sandwich. He didn't notice that the other kids had a tough time finishing theirs as well.

Nervous or not, the group was soon back in the canoes, heading straight across the lake on the last part of their trip. Michael and Eva had changed positions in their canoe. Eva was now in the stern, steering. Michael was the power paddler in front. But he didn't feel like he had power. He felt weak with fear.

Remembering the story had made Tyler nervous, too. He looked at the wide stretch of lake in front of them. He could barely see the opposite shore. "How long will it take us to get to Camp Outback?" he asked.

"It usually takes an hour and a half," Amy said. "But the lake seems a little rough now, so it could be longer."

Amy and Jeremy had noticed the change in the water earlier, when Michael did. Before they left the last campsite, they had talked about it quietly. They decided it shouldn't worry them too much. The sky was clear, and the group was made up of good, strong canoeists. A little wave now and then wouldn't hurt.

At first, the group cut through the water pretty quickly. In 10 or 15 minutes, the canoes were far out into the lake. Michael was still deep in the grip of terror, but at least strength had returned to his arms and chest. Soon, he and Eva were leading the group again.

Then Michael noticed clouds in the west, the direction they were heading. As strong as his fears were, he still wouldn't show them. That wasn't what he was about.

It was Tyler who first said something. "I hope those clouds don't mean bad weather."

"I doubt it," Jeremy said. "The forecast said it might rain late tonight, but not before then."

As Jeremy said that, the wind picked up, and the waves got stronger. The kids paddled harder toward the graying sky. Within ten minutes, the sky was completely cloudy, and the western sky looked dark.

Michael paddled grimly. He had expected the worst. It looked as if he might get it.

The canoeists were quiet as the wind got stronger and the waves got bigger. A sudden wave raised the canoes a foot high. Eva gasped in surprise. When the canoes dropped, Michael's fears didn't go away. Now he wasn't alone in his fears, either.

"Amy, is this getting dangerous?" Kara asked. Amy and Jeremy's canoes were alongside each other. The counselors exchanged worried glances that they hoped the kids didn't see.

"I don't think so," Amy said carefully. "The lake might get rougher, but if that's a storm coming, we'll beat it."

The lake did get rougher. The rich, blue water of the morning was dark and gray. The waves came faster and higher. They had white, foamy tops. The canoes bounced up and down.

"I'm getting seasick," Tyler moaned.

Even the counselors were fearful. Amy said, "We could turn around, but we're near the halfway point. It's smarter to keep going."

"I agree," Jeremy said.

"This is scary," Eva said softly.

Michael surprised himself by saying calmly, "I'll dig deeper with my paddle. That will help you steer."

The canoeists were thinking about Tyler's story. They were hoping that the weather wouldn't worsen. With the waves splashing and the paddles kicking up water, the six didn't realize that it had started to rain. Then, when bigger drops came faster and faster, they knew they were fighting a real storm.

Soon they were paddling through driving rain. The powerful wind blew sheets of water into their faces. The first flash of lightning and burst of thunder scared everyone.

"Lightning!" Jeremy cried. "If we can get to shore quickly, we should try."

"We're in the middle of the lake!" Amy yelled. "There's no fast way back to shore."

Four campers and two counselors were seriously frightened. But no one felt more fear than Michael. None of the other canoeists had almost drowned last spring.

Michael knew that fear wouldn't help. He paddled on. The waves were much rougher, bouncing each canoe higher. Rain and waves poured into the canoes, making them more difficult to handle. The powerful wind blew into the canoeists with amazing force. The pouring rain made it hard to see.

"This isn't going to work," Jeremy yelled over the roaring storm.

Kara said, "I have an idea!"

Just then the wind
roared. Great waves broke
over the boats. The canoes spun
sideways. In a single horrible instant,
everyone's fears came true. The waves picked
up a canoe and turned it upside-down!

CHAPTER 5

NO TIME TO THINK

The boat that had been flipped over was Jeremy and Kara's canoe. Kara bobbed up and down in the storm-torn waves. "Help!" she yelled. Jeremy was nowhere to be seen. Their canoe, upside-down in the water, drifted away from the others. The paddles were lost.

Amy sprang into action. From the stern of her canoe, she yelled, "Dig hard, Tyler!" Tyler paddled hard. His strong pulls allowed Amy to turn their canoe quickly. She aimed for Kara. Soon Tyler and Amy were next to her.

Amy reached over and tried to grab Kara by the life jacket. The first try missed.

The second try also missed. But on the third try, Amy got her. She pulled Kara next to the canoe. Kara clung safely to its side.

Then Amy started yelling, "Jeremy! Jeremy!"

While Amy and Tyler were rescuing Kara, Michael and Eva fought to prevent their boat from tipping. It took a few seconds, but teamwork got them back into control.

Lightning flashed again, and the storm raged. When Michael saw that Jeremy was missing, he knew it was time to act.

"Eva," he shouted over his shoulder. "Get us to the turned-over canoe."

"Okay, we're going left!" she yelled.

On the left side of the canoe, Eva jabbed her paddle into the water and held it. On the right side, Michael made several quick strokes. In an instant the boat turned left. Then they raced toward the capsized canoe.

"Jeremy!" Michael yelled. "Jeremy!" But Jeremy was out of sight. At first, all Michael could think of was Tyler's story and the body that still might be trapped on the bottom of the lake.

Then, Michael's memory of his own near drowning hit him. It didn't scare him this time, though. It helped him.

When they were close to the capsized canoe, Michael yelled, "Eva, hold us steady! I'm going in!"

"Wait, Mi—" Eva started to say. Before she got the words out, Michael carefully tipped himself backward into the lake. He did a quick backward somersault under the waves. He kicked his legs to get back to the surface. His life jacket helped him stay above water as he swam to the capsized canoe.

As lightning flashed and waves pushed him up and down in the water, Michael knew his life was in danger. But he was calm. He was almost certain about what had happened to Jeremy. When the canoe tipped over, Jeremy had probably hit his head on it. He might be knocked out, like Michael was last spring.

But unlike Michael then, Jeremy had on a life jacket. Michael guessed the jacket had pushed a stunned Jeremy to the surface. Michael thought Jeremy was trapped under his canoe.

At first, the storm pushed the capsized canoe farther away, but Michael's swimming strokes brought him closer and closer to it. In seconds, he grabbed it. Hanging onto the canoe, he took a deep breath. He let go and again pushed himself under the raging waters.

Michael fought the buoyancy of his life jacket to get completely under the canoe. Once under, Michael found that his guess was right. In the dark waters, he saw a body under the canoe. It was Jeremy.

Jeremy was bigger than Michael. Michael knew it would take an effort to free him. Still underwater, Michael swam away from the canoe and let himself bob to the surface of the lake.

He took a breath and yelled to Eva, "He's under the canoe!" Michael took another deep breath and for the third time slipped beneath the angry water.

He swam back under the canoe, fighting his life jacket again. He kicked up toward the canoe, grabbed Jeremy's life jacket, and pulled Jeremy deeper underwater. It was hard, but he brought Jeremy down with him. He pulled them both a few feet from under the canoe.

Once clear, Michael got a better hold of Jeremy's life jacket and kicked toward the surface. This time, the life jackets helped.

As the two boys broke through the top of the water, Michael gasped for air. To Michael's surprise, Jeremy did, too. He was conscious, but he had a bump on his forehead.

"What happened?" Jeremy asked, coughing out water.

"Your canoe flipped over, but you're safe now," said Michael. He didn't want Jeremy to panic.

Eva had brought their canoe close to the capsized one. In the rain and waves, Michael managed to push Jeremy into their canoe.

Michael hung on to the side for a few seconds as he caught his breath. He saw that Amy and Tyler had gotten Kara safely aboard their boat.

But before he climbed back into his canoe, Michael had one more decision to make.

CHAPTER 6

STILL A LONG WAY TO GO

Michael hung on to the edge of his canoe. He felt fear for the first time since the wave hit, but he fought it. The need for action allowed him to put it on hold.

Should I save the capsized canoe? he asked himself.

The lightning had stopped, but the storm still raged. It would be dangerous to save the canoe. It would also be dangerous to paddle to safety in these high waves with three people in each of the two remaining canoes. Besides, the canoes were filling with water from the rain and crashing waves.

Michael decided. "Let's get that canoe," he yelled to Eva. 𝄾

Eva paddled while Michael hung on to their canoe. He helped move it by kicking his legs.

They quickly reached the bobbing, capsized canoe. Michael moved to the other side of their canoe. He held it as level as he could in the rough water, while the dazed Jeremy reached over to hold the tipped-over boat.

Eva grabbed the other end of the capsized canoe. As Jeremy let go, Eva turned her end at an angle. She slowly tugged the end of the capsized canoe out of the water and across their canoe. It was hard in the terrible storm, but she pulled one canoe over the top of the other. Eva stopped pulling when she had the capsized boat sitting across the middle of their canoe.

Eva then turned over the capsized boat. With Michael's help, she slipped it back into the water. Michael carefully pulled himself out

of the water and into the empty canoe. Eva handed him a paddle. Michael quickly used it to steady the canoe in the stormy waves.

For the moment, they were safe. But the storm didn't look as if it would let up soon, and the canoeists were in bad shape. They were all soaked, and one had a head injury. All six were very, very tired. 🕯

Kara yelled over the storm, "Now it's time for my idea. Tyler, do you have the pieces of rope you found? We can tie the canoes together."

It was tricky in the driving rain and bouncing waves, but Tyler and Amy brought their canoe along one side of the canoe Michael was in. Eva guided her canoe to the other side. The canoeists tied the canoes together by the seats. Then, Kara climbed into the middle canoe with Michael.

Bound together, the three boats handled the waves and wind much better. Jeremy was dizzy. The others helped him into the center boat. Michael moved back into the canoe with Eva.

With two paddlers in front and two in back, the new triple canoe cut through the waves. About an hour later than expected, the tired group docked at Camp Outback. They were greeted with the cheers of campers waiting anxiously for their return.

The next night, under the clearest of skies, campers from both camps sat together at the campfire at Camp Outback. This was a night to honor the six heroes of the day before. Michael was singled out. He had put his own life in danger to save Jeremy.

At the end of the evening, Michael and Tyler sat up high on the hill again.

Michael stared out at East Lake. He realized he was no longer living in fear. That night in May, in a stunned state, he did panic. Yesterday was different. Yes, he was very afraid then. But he did what he had to do, and he did it well.

He sat with a smile on his face.

"Why are you smiling?" Tyler asked.

Michael looked at Tyler. "Just thinking about next year. Maybe I'll win the prize for the best 'Save Our Lake' craft," he joked.

Michael was proud of himself, but he wasn't going to tell anyone, not even Tyler. That wasn't what Michael was all about.